T0065257

30
DAYS
of Darkness

30 DAYS

of Darkness

The story of Johan and Ella

Jonathan Lopez

30 DAYS OF DARKNESS
THE STORY OF JOHAN AND ELLA

This is a work of fiction. All of the characters, names, incidents, organizations, and dialogue in this novel are either the products of the author's imagination or are used fictitiously.

iUniverse books may be ordered through booksellers or by contacting:

iUniverse
1663 Liberty Drive
Bloomington, IN 47403
www.iuniverse.com
844-349-9409

Because of the dynamic nature of the Internet, any web addresses or links contained in this book may have changed since publication and may no longer be valid. The views expressed in this work are solely those of the author and do not necessarily reflect the views of the publisher, and the publisher hereby disclaims any responsibility for them.

Any people depicted in stock imagery provided by Getty Images are models, and such images are being used for illustrative purposes only.
Certain stock imagery © Getty Images.

Unless otherwise indicated, all scripture quotations are from The Holy Bible, English Standard Version® (ESV®). Copyright ©2001 by Crossway Bibles, a division of Good News Publishers. Used by permission. All rights reserved.

ISBN: 978-1-6632-2619-8 (sc)
ISBN: 978-1-6632-2620-4 (e)

Library of Congress Control Number: 2021914154

Print information available on the last page.

iUniverse rev. date: 07/28/2021

Contents

About the Author

Jonathan Lopez was born in Puerto Rico in 1988. Jonathan has been working in the Military for 9.5 years and a local Sheriff's Office for over 6 years. In 2019 Jonathan published his first book "21 Days Myth" rated 5 stars on Amazon, Barnes & Noble and more. He moved from Puerto Rico to the states in 2013, started from zero and is continuously building a legacy to include a Firearms Academy called "E&O Tactical" and a Non-Profit Organization to assist the community with job assistance. Jonathan is a father of one boy, he is always creating a positive atmosphere to those around him. The power of words and inspirational stories are part of this book to help you in your journey to success regardless of the darkest times, this book presents a story of hardship and depression; it gives you ways on how to cope and overcome the worst. Jonathan has been awarded on several occasions for his selfless actions. Some of his awards and recognitions are The Melbourne regional Chamber Valor Award in 2018, Sheriff's Office Merit Award in 2017 and the Army Commendation Medal in 2016.

30 DAYS
of Darkness

◆　◆　◆

Chapter 1

Before the Darkness

Introduction

B efore the darkness? The darkness can be described as a bad experience, a time where your dreams seem to crumble down, your goals seem too far from you, and everything you have accomplished in life is over. It is extremely important to understand that the dark feeling and the pain is temporary. I always refer to a problem using the camera/flashlight concept, when we have a situation it is normal to naturally zoom-in or spotlight the bad situation. It is ok and acceptable to do that, however it is our responsibility to zoom out the camera and spotlight as soon as we can, otherwise we will remain in that situation for a longer period of time; probably more than what the situation deserves.

In the next pages we will share the story of Johan and Ella, key points to remember:

- Not everything that shines is gold
- No dark time is permanent

You were born to thrive and conquer, know your place.

Chapter 1

Before the Darkness

Johan was a community leader, goal oriented and a successful person in different careers and businesses; a loving father, a caring husband and a passionate individual; he was not a perfect person but was always striving to improve himself in every aspect always giving 100%.

Johan was married for more than a decade, the couple made a few mistakes during the 12-year relationship that affected the marriage in a way that trust and communication was no longer present. The best part from this relationship was a beautiful baby girl named Lilith. After 12 years he got divorced but maintained a healthy relationship with his ex-wife for the benefit of the baby.

Johan was barely getting up from his divorce that took everything from him. Starting from zero was not an obstacle with his resilient character; one kid and a new beginning, it was not the first time that Johan started from zero, the challenges in the past only made him stronger.

"I Am Not What Happened to Me. I Am What I Choose to Become"

Almost a year after his divorced Johan started a new job where the majority of employees are males, it wasn't hard to spot Ella; a young beautiful girl with an amazing smile, one look at her eyes and he was flying in the clouds. Beautiful blonde hair, green eyes where he could see the milky way galaxy and, a bubbly and happy attitude that could only bring joy and happiness. Lunch break bell went off…. Johan went to the break room and opened his lunch box with a simple sandwich and a soda, as he is getting the stuff out of the lunch box he looked up and Ella decided to sit right across the table.

Johan: "How are you?" (with a nervous tone)

Ella: "I'm better now that I'm talking to you"

Apparently, Johan wasn't the only one attracted to that "Angel", it was a mutual attraction. The chemistry during the conversation made it feel like they knew each other for a long time.

The question was:

Would it be possible to date someone that works under you, being her supervisor, same friends and same coworkers?

It was not easy, because even though he was "technically speaking" over her, it was not a direct subordinate/boss situation.

They became friends, it wasn't that hard; becoming a good friend with someone you work with, since sometimes the long hours at work are more than the time you spend at home. Johan was going through a difficult time, but Ella sparked a happiness inside his heart that he couldn't even understand.

Johan was in shock, "why me? I'm older than her, I am divorced and with a kid, most woman will consider this "baggage" this must be an illusion"

Johan couldn't believe the fact that a beautiful young blonde girl was falling for him. Meanwhile she was always around or checking on him via text or as simple as a phone call. After a few weeks of conversation, they finally got their first date, that ended up with breakfast in the morning as a typical Hollywood movie.

Ella: "You're different, this is more than a one-night thing, no one ever cooked for me before"

Once he realized that she was seeing him as something beyond a simple friendship he started pushing her away. He was convinced that the situation was surreal, he was burning in pain from his divorced and losing the home he built and this beauty was continuously present in a way that made it look like it was not real and that Ella would wake up one realizing that she could have someone better.

John: "You don't want this Ella, I'm almost 10 years older than you, I have a kid and a divorce in my history, you deserve someone young like you, someone that can match your energy, that is not going to be 60 when you are not even 49 you deserve better"

Ella: "I know what I want, and all I want is you, no one else. I can be myself when I'm around you, you make me laugh and extremely happy, I'll show you how much I love you, I will show you how love looks like"

That was the first time Ella expressed her feelings towards Johan. He was extremely confused thinking that she was wrong and that this was not possible. Dating here, dating there, seems like Chicken wings from Buffalo Wild Wings and Corona with Lime was the perfect dating meal. She was a simple and humble girl, down to earth and showing him that he was important; she became the light he needed during the stressful situation he was going through; or at least that's what he thought.

"Whoever walks in integrity walks securely, but he who makes his ways crooked will be found out." – Proverbs 10:9 (ESV-Bible, 2001)

Months passed by and they seemed to be perfect, even other people were using them as an example of love, and as an example of what a good relationship should look like. Going to some theme parks together while staying in local hotels and enjoying every single minute. Christmas lights in downtown while holding hands every second.

Johan started to believe that he found his perfect match, someone loving and caring not only about him but his kid as well.

Finally, the big day arrived, Johan was getting ready to meet Ella's parents. A little bit over an hour drive, driving through a few county lines; some cologne and a nice haircut, looking great for the most expected day. A lot of questions were placed on the table and as always Johan just opened his heart with her family as he did with Ella. Her parents were very supportive and sweet, an amazing family. Johan started to believe in love again; every time Ella held his hand was like a round trip to heaven.

Ella got to meet his kid and it went so great, a kid that is normal shy, opened up with her like she was in her life since she was born, it was an amazing and great impact seeing them playing and having a connection that cannot be ignored. Johan was falling deeply in love with Ella to the point that all questions and hesitations were dying.

30 DAYS

of Darkness

◆ ◆ ◆

Chapter 2

Darkness Began

Chapter 2

Darkness Began

Ella made promises that Johan never heard before, not even taken from a book or a movie, it was surreal. Johan has been through hell and Ella appeared to be an angel in disguise. Johan would do anything for her, anything she asked Johan did, no questions asked. Head over heels are words that cannot explain the way Johan felt. But the unexpected dark times were coming.

Ella: "Hey babe I found a job, but I need to move down closer to it and for other personal reasons"

Johan: "Don't worry love, I have space for you at home and the dating now can be everyday if you want"

Due to the career opportunity and the love Johan felt for Ella they moved in together, what an upgrade! now the "dating" was a daily amazing connection; everything was so natural. Ella would cook spontaneously some days and Johan the others. Laundry, cooking and cleaning didn't need a schedule because they were working as a team.

Late night movies and snacks, date nights every other day and quality time with the baby girl. A natural team, no arguments, no fights and any disagreement were handled with love and understanding until Johan started noticing a few things that were not concerning at the beginning but started to raise red flags.

Ella was enjoying her new job and was normally leaving for work about 40 minutes earlier to arrive on a good time considering the 25 minutes' drive. Suddenly a week later Ella started to leave the house almost an hour earlier and slowly increased where 3 weeks into the job she was leaving 2 hours earlier (before shift). Johan did not want to think negatively and wanted to give the benefit of the doubt, so he asked.

John: "Hey love, why are you leaving so early baby"

Ella: "I just like to be there on time and that covers anything, just in case there's traffic, etc.

It was a Wednesday, Ella left the house and forgot to sign out her social media account...

"Beep, beep!" The computer notification was going off continuously. Johan went to check the computer to find out that more than several individuals were engaged in a lovely conversation that made all of Ella's sweet words sound like venom and lies. Ella being young and full of life started to talk to other guys at work. With only a few weeks on the job Ella was already flirting and having strong conversation, the ones considered "sexting" with multiple coworkers.

Johan was extremely confused and for a second looked like he was living a nightmare, the worst part is that one of the individuals on the chat he once considered a brother. Johan took pictures of the conversation and contacted his "friend" about the conversation found and everything started going downhill. But what Johan didn't know is that it was only the beginning.

Without any other further contact with Ella (since she was working); hours passed by, and Johan was contacted by a detective asking if they could meet to get a statement.

Johan immediately agreed to see the detective thinking that something bad happened. The detective arrived at Johan's house and the dark time was getting closer and closer...

Detective Will: "My name is Detective Will and I need to get a statement from you"

Johan was extremely confused not knowing or understanding what was going on. The Detective read his rights:

Detective Will: *"You have the right to remain silent. Anything you say can be used against you in court. You have the right to talk to a lawyer for advice before we ask you any questions. You have the right to have a lawyer with you during questioning. If you cannot afford a lawyer, one will be appointed for you before any questioning if you wish. If you decide to answer questions now without a lawyer present, you have the right to stop answering at any time."*

Johan couldn't even speak; he was extremely confused about the whole thing not understanding anything; he was told that she wasn't allowed to go back to the house; Johan spoke with the Detective and asked him if he can explain what is going on.

Detective Will: "I am sorry I cannot disclose any information unless you want to give me a statement..."

Johan coming from a law enforcement family stated that he will provide a statement with his attorney present. The detective closed the interview, and no other details were provided. Ella was dismissed from work and allowed to go one more time to the house to get her belongings with an officer present. That was the most painful process Johan ever experienced during what we can call now a "break-up" both Johan and Ella were instructed not to contact each other, something that Ella failed to do within the first few days. Johan declined her call and refused to reply her text stating "Can we meet, can we talk..."

30 Days of silence, pain and darkness... but how Johan overcame this situation? He was not only getting depressed for the break-up but for the way it happened where they never got to have closure, his friends and coworkers were involved and that he didn't know why law enforcement

was part of the situation. It took 30 days before Johan was able to sit down with his legal representative and the detectives that originally wanted to get a statement.

In the next chapter Johan overcame the situation and learned details that were mind-blowing.

Chapter 3

Overcoming the Darkness

Chapter 3

─────◆─────

Overcoming the Darkness

F inally, the decision day arrived; the end of the investigation where Johan found out the outcome and the "evidence" was presented to him before his statement was made. While hearing and reading the evidence he basically did not have to defend himself, after being in the "unknown" for an entire month falling into depression the light was finally at the end of the tunnel.

For his surprise Ella made false allegations but when it became official, she made important changes. Detectives were called after she stated that Johan was suicidal; when the detectives arrived, she changed the accusation and stated "He hit me..." Of course, Johan didn't know until 30 days later when he was cleared from all false allegations and was able to listen to Ella's recorded statement. The worst 30 days sitting in the darkness, in the unknown, that was the worst feeling ever.

Ella hesitated every word stated, not knowing how to answer and clearly making things up on the spot. Even with a simple question Ella stutter every syllable and was going back and forward like she could not make her mind up. From "suicidal" statement to "um um ahh he heeee hit me"

Detective: "Can you be specific, how did he hit you and where? Was it with an open hand or..?"

Ella: "umm, uhh … wiiiith an open hand"

Detective: "on what part of your body?"

Ella: "uhhh ummmm iiiiin my shoulder"

None of her statements were cleared, anyone, even someone without experience could've spotted the lies behind her voice trying to hurt a man that only did good to her and just because of her desire to be with other people simultaneously.

All the promises Ella made to Johan were thrown away like it meant nothing. Those texts stating "thank you for giving me the life I always dreamed about" were just a bluff in Ella's game. Almost destroying a good man over some games from a young girl that didn't know what she wanted.

After 30 days in the Darkness Johan found out a few interesting facts:

- She was talking to 3 coworkers one being Johan's friend, someone he considered a brother

- Johan's "friend" was the one that got her to lie and the main reason of why Law Enforcement got involved

- 2 of the 3 individuals she was talking to were in a relationship (1 married, 1 engaged)

When she lied to the officers, she messed up by first calling cops for 1 reason but when they showed up she already changed her story.

30 DAYS
of Darkness

◆　◆　◆

Chapter 4

Readings of Sanity

Chapter 4

———•◦•———

Readings of Sanity

The following readings kept Johan sane during his walk-through hell, frustration and dark times:

The Way of Love

1 If I speak in the tongues of men and of angels, but have not love, I am a noisy gong or a clanging cymbal. 2 And if I have prophetic powers, and understand all mysteries and all knowledge, and if I have all faith, so as to remove mountains, but have not love, I am nothing. 3 If I give away all I have, and if I deliver up my body to be burned, but have not love, I gain nothing.

4 Love is patient and kind; love does not envy or boast; it is not arrogant 5 or rude. It does not insist on its own way; it is not irritable or resentful; 6 it does not rejoice at wrongdoing, but rejoices with the truth. 7 Love bears all things, believes all things, hopes all things, endures all things.

8 Love never ends. As for prophecies, they will pass away; as for tongues, they will cease; as for knowledge, it will pass away. 9 For we know in part and we prophesy in part, 10 but when the perfect comes, the partial will pass away. 11 When I was a child, I spoke like a child, I thought like a child, I reasoned like a child. When I became a man, I gave up childish ways. 12 For now we see in a mirror dimly, but then face to face. Now I know in part; then I shall know fully, even as I have been fully known.

13 So now faith, hope, and love abide, these three; but the greatest of these is love. 1 Corinthians 13 (ESV-Bible, 2001)

God Is Love

7 Beloved, let us love one another, for love is from God, and whoever loves has been born of God and knows God. 8 Anyone who does not love does not know God, because God is love. 9 In this the love of God was made manifest among us, that God sent his only Son into the world, so that we might live through him. 10 In this is love, not that we have loved God but that he loved us and sent his Son to be the propitiation for our sins. 11 Beloved, if God so loved us, we also ought to love one another. 12 No one has ever seen God; if we love one another, God abides in us and his love is perfected in us.

13 By this we know that we abide in him and he in us, because he has given us of his Spirit. 14 And we have seen and testify that the Father has sent his Son to be the Savior of the world. 15 Whoever confesses that

Jesus is the Son of God, God abides in him, and he in God. 16 So we have come to know and to believe the love that God has for us. God is love, and whoever abides in love abides in God, and God abides in him. 17 By this is love perfected with us, so that we may have confidence for the day of judgment, because as he is so also are we in this world. 18 There is no fear in love, but perfect love casts out fear. For fear has to do with punishment, and whoever fears has not been perfected in love. 19 We love because he first loved us. 20 If anyone says, "I love God," and hates his brother, he is a liar; for he who does not love his brother whom he has seen cannot love God whom he has not seen. 21 And this commandment we have from him: whoever loves God must also love his brother. 1 John 4:7-21 (ESV-Bible, 2001)

My Refuge and My Fortress

1 He who dwells in the shelter of the Most High
will abide in the shadow of the Almighty.
2 I will say to the Lord, "My refuge and my fortress,
my God, in whom I trust."
3 For he will deliver you from the snare of the fowler
and from the deadly pestilence.
4 He will cover you with his pinions,
and under his wings you will find refuge;
his faithfulness is a shield and buckler.

5 You will not fear the terror of the night,

nor the arrow that flies by day,

6 nor the pestilence that stalks in darkness,

nor the destruction that wastes at noonday.

7 A thousand may fall at your side,

ten thousand at your right hand,

but it will not come near you.

8 You will only look with your eyes

and see the recompense of the wicked.

9 Because you have made the Lord your dwelling place—

the Most High, who is my refuge—

10 no evil shall be allowed to befall you,

no plague come near your tent.

11 For he will command his angels concerning you

to guard you in all your ways.

12 On their hands they will bear you up,

lest you strike your foot against a stone.

13 You will tread on the lion and the adder;

the young lion and the serpent you will trample underfoot.

14 "Because he holds fast to me in love, I will deliver him;

I will protect him, because he knows my name.

15 When he calls to me, I will answer him;

I will be with him in trouble;

I will rescue him and honor him.

16 With long life I will satisfy him

and show him my salvation."

Psalm 91 (ESV-Bible, 2001)

21 Days Myth – (Chapter 2)

"It's important to understand this concept and start to change our viewpoint as things happen to us. Sometimes we are in control of certain situations, and sometimes we need to adapt and overcome a situation that we did not want or could not control anymore.

You have the power to decide where you're going to be in the next year, in the next 5 years, and in the next 10, but you will need to visualize your goals, write them down, and develop a plan. Don't expect to get there in a day, but make sure you do something. Whether it's something big or small, make sure there is something for you to work on that will bring you closer to that goal and dream. Sometimes we cannot avoid certain situations, but we can certainly control our reactions to each situation.

Establishing a vision is very important; you need to know what you want, then you can start doing everything you can to move you closer to that vision.

Identifying your weakness and strengths is another big step to take during your journey. Listening to the people around you for good quality constructive criticism.Choosecriticism. Choose wisely; listen to hose that always bring something good to the table. If someone is talking about how to improve your credit score, that person should have a great credit score 700+. Keep in mind, though that you cannot listen to everyone's opinion because you will never be able to please everyone.

Credibility is one of the filters you need to apply to analyze the people around you. Use that credibility filter to know which advice you should listen to. Another helpful thing you can do is make a list of the strengths and weaknesses that you know you have. Then ask people that are close to you (family, good friends, supporters) what they think you should do to improve as a person. Sometimes it's good to know how our whole picture looks from the outside and from others' point of view. In the military, we used the term AAR (After Actions Review). This was conducted after every training or mission. This type of review helps to keep up the good things about ourselves and avoid repeating mistakes in the future. It's not like you are going to hold yourself back because someone doesn't share the same vision as you do, but it's a helpful thing to see yourself how others see you.

How many times someone do you hear someone complaining about a task you love to do?

How many times do you hear someone complaining about something you consider a blessing?

Perspective is always a great thing to keep in mind because it is always good to receive some kind of counseling from a friend, a mentor, or family member to help us see and understand their different points of view.

Make sure you surround yourself with people that are open minded, successful, and an inspiration to others. There's an old saying that says, "You're a product of who you surround yourself with." Make sure you cover that in your mental checklist. During this process, you will find out that sometimes family become strangers and strangers become family. Keep in mind that you might know how to execute a mission, but if your plan isn't right, you'll fail. On the other hand, you might know how to develop a plan without knowing how to start. These two concepts are meant to be together; work on both of them and make sure you have a mentor with the right experience to guide you." (Lopez, 2019, p. 21 Days Myth)

The Lord Is My Shepherd

A Psalm of David.

1 The Lord is my shepherd; I shall not want.

2 He makes me lie down in green pastures.

He leads me beside still waters.

3 He restores my soul.

He leads me in paths of righteousness

for his name's sake.

4 Even though I walk through the valley of the shadow of death,

I will fear no evil,

for you are with me;

your rod and your staff,

they comfort me.

5 You prepare a table before me

in the presence of my enemies;

you anoint my head with oil;

my cup overflows.

6 Surely goodness and mercy shall follow me

all the days of my life,

and I shall dwell in the house of the Lord

forever. Psalms 23 (ESV-Bible, 2001)

30
DAYS
of Darkness

◆　◆　◆

Chapter 5

Remain Resilient

Chapter 5

Remain Resilient

resiliency

1. the capacity to recover quickly from difficulties, toughness.

   "the often-remarkable resilience of so many British institutions"

2. the ability of a substance or object to spring back into shape; elasticity.

   "nylon is excellent in wearability and resilience"

(Dictionary, p. Oxford)

At the end of the day resiliency must be exercised in order to continuously develop the skill. Icebergs are known for only exposing the tip above the water level, but they are bigger underneath. Two key components that we must understand are:

1. Good Icebergs

2. Bad Icebergs

Examples of those icebergs in the next few pages.

What are good icebergs?

For this example, I will use a successful person, or success itself. People tend to see success in someone's ability to reach their goals and don't understand everything that happens behind closed doors.

The following picture is a good example of a goof iceberg:

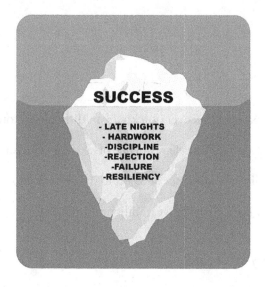

In the other hand we have bad icebergs, for this example we will use "Depression" people only see the constant sadness and often they can't understand what is the foundation.

The following picture is a good example of a bad iceberg:

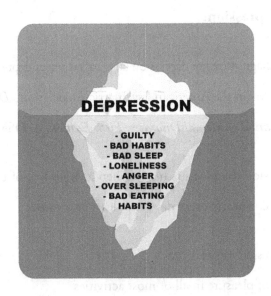

Depression is often misunderstood as just feeling sad. But it's a complex medical condition thought to be caused by a combination of factors, including genetic, biological, psychological, and environmental triggers, according to the National Institute of Mental Health (NIMH). While it's not yet clear exactly what causes depression, researchers have made great progress in learning more about how to manage and treat this common mental health disorder. Here are some facts about depression, depression symptoms, and depression management that might surprise you.

What Is Depression?

Doctors diagnose major depression (also called major depressive disorder) based on criteria in the American Psychiatric Association's *Diagnostic and Statistical Manual of Mental Disorders, Fifth Edition*, or DSM-V.

A depression diagnosis is made when at least five of the following symptoms occur nearly every day for at least two weeks:

- Depressed mood
- Loss of pleasure in all or most activities
- Significant weight change or change in appetite
- Change in sleep
- Change in activity
- Fatigue or loss of energy
- Diminished concentration
- Feelings of guilt or worthlessness
- Thoughts of suicide

To diagnose major depression, either depressed mood or loss of pleasure in activities must be one of the symptoms.

12 Things You Might Not Know About Depression

While the definition of major depression may seem simple enough, depression has profound and varying impacts. Here are some facts about depression that everyone may not know.

1. **Depression has different triggers.** People have a higher risk of depression if they've recently been through a stressful life event; if they've had depression in the past; or if a close family member has been depressed. Sometimes depression develops without any obvious cause.

2. **Genes provide some (but not all) of the answers.** The genetic predisposition to depression is becoming better understood and might explain why one person becomes depressed and another doesn't, says Ole Thienhaus, MD, a professor of psychiatry at the University of Arizona College of Medicine in Tucson. A family history of depression matters, but it's not always the only factor. For example, the heritability rate — the percentage of a trait that may be due to genes — of depression is only about 37 percent, according to a study published in July 2018 in the journal *Frontiers in Psychiatry*.

3. **Depression affects the body.** Headache, stomach problems, headaches, and general aches and pains without a clear physical cause can all be symptoms of depression, according to the NIMH.

4. **Depression might be a "gut feeling."** A study published in August 2020 in the journal *Cureus* found a strong connection between gut health and mental well-being, noting that depression is strongly associated with gut imbalance. A varied diet including probiotics and prebiotics may play a role in managing depression, although more research is needed.

5. **Depressed brains may look different.** Some people with major depressive disorder have changes in the brain that can be seen in imaging tests such as magnetic resonance imaging (MRI) scans, according to a review published in December 2019 in the journal *Translational Psychiatry* that evaluated studies examining the use of MRI scans to diagnose and treat major depressive disorder. (That said, the paper also notes that major depression is a biologically complex disorder that causes different changes in the brain in some people, and that MRI scans alone are not useful in the diagnosis of major depressive disorder; the researchers therefore state the importance of new imaging techniques and ways of analyzing that information to help diagnose depression.)

6. **Depression is linked to other health problems.** People with depression are also at higher risk of chronic inflammatory or autoimmune conditions such as diabetes, heart disease, arthritis, or irritable bowel disease. It's unclear if depression causes inflammation or vice versa, according to a study published in July 2019 in the journal *Frontiers in Immunology*.

7. **Depressed people might not look depressed.** "Depression is a hidden illness," says Jeremy Coplan, MD, a professor of psychiatry at the State University of New York (SUNY) Downstate Medical Center in Brooklyn. Some people can seem upbeat and cheerful, but inside they're struggling with the symptoms of depression.

8. **Exercise can help manage depression.** "Exercise improves mood state," says Dr. Thienhaus, who explains that exercise helps stimulate natural compounds in the body that can make you feel better. Aim for at least 30 minutes of physical activity most days. "We typically recommend that people with depression exercise, develop a healthy diet, and go to bed at a regular time." A study published in October 2017 in the *American Journal of Psychiatry* found that even one hour of physical activity each week was associated with a 12 percent lower incidence of depression.

9. **It's common to need to try more than one antidepressant.** Many people with depression don't get relief from the first antidepressant they try. That is expected because for unknown reasons, different people benefit from different medications, and some don't find any benefit from medications we currently have available. According to Diane Solomon, PhD, a psychiatric nurse practitioner in Portland, Oregon, people may sometimes need to try several medication before they find an antidepressant that works well for them.

10. **Therapy is usually needed, too.** For mild to moderate depression, therapy and lifestyle changes are considered first-line; however,

for moderate to severe depression, a combination of therapy and medication is often helpful. Sometimes antidepressant medications will be used first to alleviate depression enough for therapy to be helpful, Dr. Coplan says. But psychotherapy, cognitive behavioral therapy, or other therapeutic strategies, such as transcranial magnetic stimulation, are also needed for effective depression treatment.

11. **Depression is often experienced with coexisting anxiety.** Many people who have one mental health disorder, such as depression, may experience another, such as anxiety or attention deficit hyperactivity disorder. "Anxiety can be as debilitating as depression, but people may have lived with it so long, they don't realize they actually have anxiety," says Dr. Solomon, who adds that women are especially vulnerable to anxiety disorders.

12. **Depression profoundly affects people throughout the world.** A February 2017 report from the World Health Organization stated that depression is the leading cause of disability in the world, affecting more than 300 million people worldwide. It also showed an 18 percent increase between 2005 and 2015 in the number of people living with depression, the majority of whom are young people, elderly people, and women.

Depression Resources

Many organizations also have online resources for depression, including:

- NIMH

- National Alliance on Mental Illness

- American Psychological Association

- Depression and Bipolar Support Alliance

- Anxiety and Depression Association of America

If you're struggling with suicidal thoughts, go to your nearest emergency room or contact the National Suicide Prevention Lifeline at 800-273-8255 (TALK).

For help finding a therapist, call the Substance Abuse and Mental Health Services Administration (SAMSA)'s National Helpline at 1-800-662-HELP (4357) for a free, confidential referral for treatment. (Madeline R. Vann, 2021)

SUCCESS!

The first thing I recommend is to define success, generally speaking the dictionary definition of "Success" is:

the accomplishment of an aim or purpose.

"there is a thin line between success and failure"

1. ARCHAIC

the good or bad outcome of an undertaking.

"the good or ill success of their maritime enterprises"

(Dictionary, p. Oxford)

But you need to define success in your life, i.e.

- For a teacher that is happy with the job, success is seeing the students complete their scholar year, could be as simple as 100% passing their grade or someone competing in a city/state event representing not only the class but the school
- For a police officer could be helping their local community, completing 20 years of service maybe without any injuries and/or use of force that took someone's life
- Could be getting married and having a family and/or the opposite, remain single and focused on their career

The list can go on and is almost infinite but defining what you consider "success" is an important task and should be 100% clear. No one including yourself can judge your "successful" life, that is up to you and what makes you happy.

At the end you must understand that your past cannot define your future, you are destined to break "generational curses", to build a legacy and shine in everything you do, I encourage you to never back down, it is ok a temporary pause, it is healthy to stay still for a moment specially during an adverse situation but NEVER!!! NEVER!!! Camp there, never moved or live in that pause, it is meant to gather facts, your thoughts and reengage, coming back stronger than never before.

Moving Forward Podcast

This podcast can be found on Spotify *(Moving Forward – Random Pad, Let's Talk)* I had the opportunity to engage the public on Random Pad, Let's Talk Podcast with Joshuwa Engelhardt.

Here a few key points:

- Don't have Random Goals, ensure the goals are clear
- Be willing to do what it takes (Commit to your goals)
- Breakdown your goals to yearly, monthly, weekly and daily, that will keep you focused on daily tasks to be accomplished towards the main goal (short, medium and long term goals = Time Management)
- Have a clear why of what you are doing, that will give you purpose, this can be applied to anything you are doing or want to do; when everything goes down you can always fall back to your purpose.
- Progress still progress, whether you are driving 5 MPH or 60 MPH, just continue to move forward.
- Have a Vision and a Mission clear
- Create Healthy Habits

Start whether you think "I am not ready" no one successful can say they were 100% ready to do what they are doing. Most of the time you will learn from your mistakes to include starting a business or raising a family

ALWAYS MOVE FORWARD!

WHAT DO YOU SEE?

1. **A number 6?**

2. **A number 9?**

3. **What is the direction of travel, right or left lane?**

After seeing the picture above anyone can argue that the answer will be based on someone's "Perspective"; but some things must be taken in consideration.

1. A number 6 maybe based on the direction of travel

2. A number 9 if that was the intent of the person who wrote the number

3. To answer the question about direction of travel, most people in the U.S. will say that vehicles should travel on the right lane, right? What if the road is in U.K.? what if they are both the same direction?

At the end of the day uninformed perspective, it is not valid, we can voice our opinion, but an opinion will never overwrite **FACTS!!**

A Fact Can be proven to be "truth"

An Opinion Can be based on emotions or perspective

It is our duty to avoid assumptions and focus on an informed opinion based on facts. By doing so our judgment will be fairly accurate in everything that surround us like, a situation we might be facing, someone's behavior, etc.

Summary

In this book I shared the fictional story of Johan and Ella with the reader to use it as an example of any possible adverse situation that people might face in their life. The key points discussed on chapter 4 and 5 will help the reader to stay focused and see the bigger picture, stress, anxiety and depression are common during the dark times but we were born to shine. Hope you enjoyed 30 Days of Darkness.

References

- Oxford Dictionary

- ESV-Bible. (2001). *The Holy Bible.* English standard version bible.

- Lopez, J. (2019). *21 Days Myth.*

- Madeline R. Vann, M. (2021, Jan 18). *Every Day Health.* Retrieved from https://www.everydayhealth.com/hs/major-depression-health-well-being/surprising-depression-facts/

Printed in the United States
by Baker & Taylor Publisher Services

Printed in the United States
by Baker & Taylor Publisher Services